# Cat and Mouse
## in the Snow

## To Hela and Janusz

ISBN 0-439-20747-9

12 11 10 9 8 7 6 5 4 3          1 2 3 4 5 6/0

Printed in the U.S.A.          09

First Scholastic printing, January 2001

Designed by Monika Keano

**Tomek Bogacki**

# Cat and Mouse
## in the Snow

SCHOLASTIC INC.

New York  Toronto  London  Auckland  Sydney
Mexico City  New Delhi  Hong Kong

**A** curious little mouse and a curious little cat
sneaked out very early one morning to play in
the green meadow, as they did every day.

**B**ut on this day the world around them looked
very different. It was all white.

"Where is the green meadow?" asked the little mouse.

"It's gone," said the little cat. "Let's find it."

**A**nd so they set out to look for the green
meadow. Up, up, up they climbed to the top
of the hill.

**T**hen, oops! The ground slipped away and down, down, down they slid.

In the meantime, the other little mice and cats woke up and went out to look for their brother and sister.

They wanted to play in the green meadow, too. But they couldn't find it, either.

"Where has it gone?" asked the little mice.
"And where is our brother?" asked the little cats.
"And our sister?" echoed the little mice.

**S**uddenly they saw two strange white creatures
right in front of them.
"Eeek," squeaked the mice. "Who are they?"
"Monsters!" screeched the cats.

**A**nd off they ran as fast as they could, up, up,
up the hill.

**T**hen, oops! The ground slipped away and
down, down, down they slid to the bottom
of the hill.

They came to a stop right next to the strange white creatures. There they sat, three mice and three cats, covered with snow.

**T**hey looked at themselves. They looked at one another, and they burst out laughing. They all looked like white monsters now.

And they knew that the green meadow hadn't gone away. It was now the snowy meadow.

**A**nd so they began to play.
They slid down the hill . . . whoosh!

**They threw snowballs . . . whee!**

**A**nd they played and played until their coats
were wet and their paws were cold.

When they came back home, they talked far
into the night about how much fun it was to
play in the snow.

And they hoped the green meadow would stay
white for a long, long time.